Dundonald Tales

Gothic fiction inspired by Scottish history

Written by

SUZY A. KELLY

Illustrated by Michael Kelly

ISBN: 978 1 9996638 0 3

First Published in Great Britain in 2018 by:

Runt Publishing
Apt 23649
Chynoweth House
Trevissome Park
Truro, TR4 8UN

For the people of Dundonald, Scotland.

SUZY A. KELLY

SUZY A. KELLY

CONTENTS

ACKNOWLEDGEMENTS

The writer and illustrator would like to thank the following people without whose kind help and support this project could not have been realised:

With many thanks to Dr Kirsteen Croll at Dundonald Castle & Visitor Centre and Mr. Jim McQuiston for all their enthusiastic help with the historical research.

Thank you to the National Trust for Scotland and the National Library of Scotland for granting us permission to reproduce portraiture and maps held in their care.

Thanks also to Dundonald Castle Creatives and Ayr Writers' Club for all their ongoing advice and encouragement.

And thank you to all our friends and Beta readers who gave their time and shared their expertise in various phases of the project. Thanks especially to the wonderful Kat Barnard, Carrie-Jennifer Cairns, Elizabeth Campbell, Joan Collinson, Alison Craig, Carole Currie, Jacqueline Currie, William Currie, Iain Gillingham, Pamela Gray, Pat Greenland, Tracy Harvey, Shirley Husband, Nicola Irving, Zoe James, Lynn Johnson, Helen Kelly, Mike Kelly, Samantha Kelly, Wendy Lothian, Rochelle McConnell, Babs Murray, Anda Nicolson, Kirsty Reid, Kirsteen Robertson, Claire Russell, Sonya Stewart, Tracey Wilson, and Tedi Young.

INTRODUCTION

This collection of short stories came to life as part of the writer's MLitt in Creative Writing at the University of Glasgow. However, the project soon developed, and we wanted to share the results of our research with a wider audience.

These stories and illustrations are therefore intended as a celebration of the village of Dundonald and its people.

THE BABA WITCH

er stepmother told her to start walking at sunset. So, as any good stepdaughter might, Lissa journeyed into the forest as the last pink rays of the sun dropped behind the horizon. Although she was almost old enough to marry, the girl kept a faded hand-sewn doll tucked inside her shirt pocket, and it scouted a safe path for her through the dense woodland.

Lissa took this special doll everywhere she went. Its eyes were brown, like her mother's, its cheeks were pink and soft, like her mother's, and its voice was just as gentle.

'Take care, dear one,' cried the cloth doll, as Lissa stumbled over roots and lost her footing.

With the river still in spate, the ground on either side of it ran deep with mud. So, trying not to get stuck, Lissa eased herself towards the river's edge and stepped along the fallen tree trunk that bridged the gap across the rushing water.

'But, Dollet,' said Lissa, as she reached the opposite bank, 'I must fetch the candles from auntie tonight. You heard what stepmother said. Get there quickly, or else the Baba Witch will…'

'You leave her to me,' tutted the doll.

Lissa smiled freely for the first time since her father had abandoned her into her stepmother's charge. She knew she could survive anything, even the terrifying, child-eating Baba Witch, as long as she had her special doll.

Dark clouds above the forest soon smothered out the daylight and Lissa's senses took a while to grow used to the threatening shapes all around her.

'Have courage, little one,' said the doll.

But Lissa did not feel brave. Every needle-like branch on every tree seemed as if it wanted to prick out her eyes.

'Keep walking,' said the doll.

***

After a few hours of watching her every step, Lissa reached the bottom of a rocky incline. She refused to walk any further in the dark.

'Can we wait here until morning?' she pleaded. 'There's no moon to guide us. I'm so tired and the stones keep crunching under my feet.'

'We can go the quickest way to fetch the candles or we can go the easiest, but,' said the doll before Lissa could answer, 'you can sleep when you reach the top of the hill. There might be wolves in this part of the forest.'

'But Dollet…' said Lissa.

'Keep climbing,' ordered the cloth doll. 'I'll tell you where to place your hands and where to dig in your feet. Trust me.'

'But, every time I think it's safe to climb a little higher, the moss comes away in my hands…look?' said Lissa, her outstretched hands full of dark, ragged clumps.

'Little one,' whispered the doll, 'those are not stones below your feet and that is not moss you are holding.'

'Then, what is it?' cried Lissa throwing it away.

'Hair.'

'Hair?'

'Although this route is the fastest, it is not the easiest. We must cross the Baba Witch's midden. Remember what she eats?'

'Oh,' cried Lissa, as she thought things over. 'This is…her leftovers?'

'Yes,' said the doll.

At the realisation, Lissa started scrambling upwards. She clawed out in front of her, desperate to secure a handhold, but she slid down the pile of children's skeletons until she was back where she started. Arm bones and hip bones cracked beneath her boots.

'Dear one, stop panicking,' said the doll. 'Remember the ritual. I can help you.'

Lissa felt her heart beating in her throat. Every instinct she had was screaming for her to run away. And yet, the little doll had never once steered her wrong.

Lissa thought back to the last time she had seen her mother alive. She had lain beside her mother's skinny frame and listened to the rasping sound her chest made when she spoke.

'Little one,' whispered the doll, 'those are not stones below your feet and that is not moss you are holding.'

'Darling one,' her mother wheezed, 'this little doll is a token of my love. Whenever you need help, do this in my memory…'

So, remembering what her mother had taught her, Lissa searched in her skirt pockets for crumbs. She gave what little she had to the cloth doll. As it fed, Lissa chanted, 'Little friend, have your feed, and help me in my time of need…'

As soon as Lissa finished the words, the doll mumbled in her ear and Lissa scaled the hill of bones as fast as a mountain goat, running and running until she reached the top.

Out of breath, Lissa lay beneath the spread of an ancient elm to recover. The cloth doll watched over her while she slept.

***

'Dear One, get up. Get up,' shouted the doll the following morning. 'Something is coming for us…'

Lissa had no time to rub her eyes. She scrambled off the track and found a hiding place just as a giant white horse charged towards her. The headless rider on its back was dressed in white armour. The horse passed by and galloped into the distance with its ears pointed forwards and its mane swirling. Neither it nor its rider noticed Lissa.

'Go now. Hurry,' said the doll after the danger had passed.

'Which path now?' asked Lissa.

'Where those hoof prints came from.'

'Really? That way?'

'Do you want to get the candles for your stepmother or not?'

'Yes, but…'

'Then start walking…'

But before the doll could finish, another giant horse charged towards them. This time, the headless rider was dressed in blood red armour and its horse was bright red from its mane to its hooves. The horse thundered straight at Lissa, churning up the dirt track as it sped along.

'Watch out,' cried the doll.

At the last moment, Lissa jumped aside and rolled into the bushes. If she had not been so quick, she would surely have been trampled. The horse and its rider galloped to the far side of the forest without acknowledging Lissa's presence.

'Now is the time for courage,' said the doll.

Lissa groaned. Still lying face down in the dirt, she knew the cloth doll was right. Like the fungus beetle crawling along beside her, she knew she would have to keep on walking.

***

Lissa spent many hours trudging through the forest, trying to avoid brambles and nettles, and stopping to eat berries. She followed the narrow path until it reached a precipice. Here, the land dropped sharply into a trickling burn. At the other side of the thin water channel, in the middle of a clearing, smoke rose from a small chimney.

'That must be Auntie's house,' said an excited Lissa.

'Wait. Wait. Let us make sure of it first,' the doll cautioned.

But Lissa was already sliding down the slope on her behind. When she reached the bottom, the sound of fiendish hooves and monstrous whinnying broke through the forest. Lissa froze with her back pressed against a large boulder. She squeezed her eyes closed, knowing what to expect this time. But as the noise grew louder and louder, she could not stop herself from opening one eye, just a little. As she did so, a velvet black horse leapt over her head. This time, the headless rider was dressed in black armour.

'That was so close,' gasped the doll as the horse's hooves cleared Lissa's nose.

'Yes, Dollet,' whispered Lissa, biting her lip.

'Well, don't just lay there panting,' said the doll. 'Go and investigate…you have candles to fetch.'

As night began, Lissa remembered her stepmother's quest. She took a deep breath and jumped across the burn. As she tiptoed towards the house in the clearing, she checked all around her for danger.

***

The smoke from the chimney smelled oddly sweet, like burning meat. But it was not the smell of any animal that Lissa's stepmother and stepsisters ate.

Up close, Lissa saw the small cottage was protected by a tall fence made of thick, sharp thorns. Rows of human skulls were embedded in each one of its fenceposts. Each skull had two fiery blue eyes that lit up the night. They followed Lissa's every move. Whenever she stepped to the right, the eyes swivelled right. Whenever she stepped to the left, the eyes swivelled left.

Lissa felt as though the skulls wanted her to reach out and touch them. As her fingertips reached to graze a cheekbone, the ground began to shake. At first, it was a gentle rumble that shook all the beech trees in the clearing. But it soon escalated into an earthquake of such violence that Lissa was knocked to the ground and the doll was thrown from her pocket.

'Dollet,' cried Lissa as she searched for her friend.

'Over here!' shouted the cloth doll.

Lissa crawled towards the sound of its comforting voice.

As she drew closer, the doll said, 'Here I am. Here I am.'

Finally, Lyssa found it.

'Oh, Dollet,' she said, scooping it up and kissing its forehead. 'What would I ever do without you?'

'Hush now,' said the doll.

When Lissa returned the cloth doll to her pocket, the earthquake was replaced by the loudest, shrillest scream that she had ever heard. Just as she thought her eardrums would burst with the noise, the Baba Witch appeared in her flying cauldron.

'I smell the blood of youth,' shrieked the witch. 'Who dares disturb this place?'

As the Baba Witch landed in the clearing, Lissa pushed herself forward and said, 'Mm…me, Auntie.'

'Mmm…me?' stammered the Baba Witch, imitating Lissa. 'Who are you and what do you want? Quickly girl, or I'll tear out your tongue.'

'Candles, Auntie. Stepmother sent me for candles…'

'Did she now?' said the Baba Witch, climbing down from her cauldron.

Glaring at Lissa, the witch removed her hat and dared Lissa to comment on her pointed, bald head. Lissa couldn't help herself and gasped.

The witch raised a thin, white eyebrow and said, 'What?'

'Nothing,' said Lissa. '…you…you have a pretty head.'

'Well,' said the Baba Witch, lifting up Lissa's cloak to see how much meat she had on her bones, 'I like to eat lying children the most.'

Lissa pulled her cloak back down. As she started to stammer again, the cloth doll tugged at her shirt pocket, encouraging her to be brave.

'Please, Auntie…' said Lissa.

'Tell me, girl,' snapped the Baba Witch. 'Are you a worker or an idler?'

'W…w…worker.'

'Are you? You have such smooth hands and perfect, soft skin.'

'Oh, but I am a hard worker. I can show you.'

'You can?' laughed the Baba Witch.

'Yes, Auntie.'

'Then you will work for me and I will give you the candles.'

'Yes, Auntie,' said Lissa, swallowing hard.

'That wasn't a question,' grunted the Baba Witch. 'Now, follow me…'

***

The Baba Witch chanted in a strange language and the thorned gate in front of the cottage began to swing open. The old witch marched on and Lissa ran along behind her, trying her best to keep up. As the huge gate swung closed, a large white horse and its rider leapt into the courtyard behind them and vanished into the mist. Soon, the blood red horse and its rider cleared the gate too, and they also disappeared into the back of the courtyard.

'Wha…what was that?' Lissa squeaked.

'What was what?' barked the Baba Witch without turning around.

'The…the huge horses and the headless…'

'The white rider was Day and the red one was the Sun.'

'What about the other one? There was a third one…'

'Night,' said the Baba Witch with an irritated sigh. 'Now, do you have any more questions? I am feeling a little hungry for…meat.'

The Baba Witch towered over Lissa and waited for a reply.

'No,' said Lissa.

'You're sure?'

'Yes.'

'Well, that is a shame…' said the Baba Witch marching off. Calling over her shoulder, she added, '…for I like to eat nosy children the most.'

Lissa did not speak, and for a second, she did not even dare to breathe.

The Baba Witch whistled, and the cottage raised itself up on two skinny legs that ended in crow's feet. Each of the black talons had black fingernails, and each fingernail looked sharp enough to disembowel a beast, or a young girl who was out in the forest, late at night, by herself.

The cottage turned around slowly to face its master. The lights switched on and then the ragged wooden door opened by itself.

'Boots off,' barked the Baba Witch as she stomped inside.

Lissa obeyed at once.

***

Flames roared in the hearth as the Baba Witch sat down in her favourite armchair. She pointed to the bare and dusty floorboards and urged Lissa to sit down next to her.

'Now, you say you're a hard worker?' said the Baba Witch.

'Yes, Auntie,' said Lissa, crossing her legs on the floor. 'I work the fields for my stepmother and stepsisters.'

'You do?'

'Yes, I till the soil and plant the seeds. Then, at harvest time, I thresh all the corn and bundle it together.'

'By yourself?' scoffed the Baba Witch. 'Where are the blisters on your palms? Where are the lines on your face from the hot sun? Why are you still so plump and round?'

The witch's dark eyes flickered when she spoke about Lissa's body. The cloth doll tugged again at Lissa's pocket, urging her to be wary of what she said next, for the cloth doll knew that the Baba Witch had little tolerance for lies.

***

Lissa thought back to the previous harvest. While her stepmother and stepsisters sat in the garden and shaded themselves beneath lace parasols, Lissa hid in the cornfield pretending to be hard at work. For instead of threshing the corn herself, Lissa fed the cloth doll the last of her stale crusts of bread.

'Little friend, have your feed, and help me in my time of need,' she sang to it.

Once the doll had finished eating, it gave Lissa a special balm to use that would protect her delicate skin from the sun and the wind. Then, while Lissa rested, the doll made sure the entire field of corn was cut and stacked in thick bunches.

When Lissa returned to the townhouse that evening, she overheard her stepmother and stepsisters complaining about her.

'How is it she can work outside all day and her skin does not burn?' said the oldest stepsister.

'Why is she not an ugly bag of bones? She doesn't eat the same fine foods that we do,' said the youngest.

'Yes,' said the stepmother, 'and how is it she can attract so many suitors? I chased another one away only this morning. I told him, "Alas, my dear stepchild is determined not to marry until both her sisters have enjoyed wedded bliss."'

***

Still angry at all her family's tricks, Lissa was determined not to do the same thing to the Baba Witch. Although, she still thought it wise not to confess the truth about the little cloth doll and its powers.

'So,' said the Baba Witch pressing Lissa for an answer. 'You received no help at all?'

'A little,' admitted Lissa with an embarrassed smile. 'But, Auntie,' she said, trying hard to change the subject, 'may I have the candles now?'

'You will get what you deserve,' said the Baba Witch, 'once you have done your work.'

'Yes, of course,' said Lissa and she held out her hand expecting the Baba Witch to shake on the agreement.

The puzzled witch yawned, but before she fell asleep she mumbled, 'I do love to eat lazy children the most…'

Lissa snatched her hand back. She curled up at the feet of the witch and slept, for the first time, with the heat of the fire on her back.

***

When Lissa awoke the next day, it took her a few moments to remember that she had not spent the previous night in the tiny cupboard that her stepmother made her sleep in after her father left. Although there was no straw mattress for her to lay on at the Baba Witch's cottage, there was room enough for her to stretch out. As she reached out her short, plump legs, she realised she did not stub her toe on the wall and that none of her muscles were cramped. Neither was her back sore from contorting into unnatural shapes all night. Taking great joy in her new freedom, Lissa smiled to herself.

Suddenly, the Baba Witch dropped a small bowl beside Lissa's head.

'Eat,' grumbled the witch, and she nudged Lissa in the ribs with her pointed slipper.

Lissa squealed. She picked up the unwashed bowl and scraped the worst of the mould off the slivers of grey meat. She ate one slice and slipped the rest into her skirt pocket.

The Baba Witch buttoned up her coat said, 'Today, you will work for me.'

'Yes, Auntie,' said Lissa.

'You will peel every potato…'

'Yes, Auntie.'

'You will wash all the linens…'

'Yes.'

'Then you will sweep out the courtyard…Are you deaf, girl? I said you will sweep out the courtyard?'

'Y…y…yes…Auntie.'

'And then you will dig up all the turnips…'

Lissa nodded, trying to hide her shock at being given such a long list of tasks.

'…and if you don't complete it all by the time I return,' growled the Baba Witch, 'I will eat you for dinner.'

'Yes, Auntie,' Lissa gulped.

With that, the witch pulled on her hat and grumbled her way out of the front door.

Lissa watched from the window as the Baba Witch's rusty cauldron flew over the trees. As the witch reached the horizon, the velvet black horse and its rider jumped over the thorned gate and vanished into the courtyard. A moment later, the white horse, the blood red horse, and their riders left the courtyard and galloped out into the forest. Lissa's work day had begun.

***

Lissa crept into the Baba Witch's tiny kitchen. She stared at all the potatoes piled up on the counter. They were almost stacked up to the roof beams and most of them were green and had sprouted long, white tendrils. Every time, Lissa peeled a potato, its skin grew back.

Lissa shook her head and tried another task. This time she opened the lid of the linen basket. But every time she pulled out a sheet, it was replaced by another. Lissa slammed the basket closed.

This time, she opened the back door and looked out into the messy courtyard. The ground that wasn't hidden by mist was ankle-deep with horse manure. Lissa shook her head again and decided to try the final task. So, she wrapped herself in the Baba Witch's shawl, which itched her skin and smelled like onions, and walked out to the vegetable patch. Lissa picked up the shovel leaning against the thorned fence and tried digging. However, every time she stamped on the shovel and removed a pile of soil, the hole filled itself up again. There was no way she could dig up one turnip, never mind all of them. There was only one thing Lissa could do now.

***

Lissa stormed inside the cottage and tapped on her shirt pocket.

'Dollet,' cried Lissa, waking up the little cloth doll. 'If I don't do what the Baba Witch wants, she will eat me for dinner tonight.'

In a patient voice, the doll replied, 'You know what to do.'

So Lissa removed the slivers of mouldy meat from her skirt pocket and fed it to the doll.

While the doll ate, Lissa sang, 'Little friend, have your feed, and help me in my time of need…'

***

The Baba Witch returned home that evening and was shocked to find every single potato had been peeled and placed in a large pot of boiling water. The linen was also folded neatly. When the old witch opened the back door, she discovered to her horror that the courtyard was spotless and that the vegetable patch was piled high with turnips.

'You did all this while I was gone?' spat the Baba Witch.

'Yes, Auntie,' said Lissa.

'Very well, I won't eat you tonight,' said the Baba Witch. 'I will have to eat something else.'

Then the old witch gave out a long sigh and sat down at her kitchen table in foul and furious mood. She shooed Lissa away and ordered her to close the kitchen door behind her. But instead of sitting cross-legged by the fireplace, Lissa spied on the witch through the keyhole.

Lissa's mouth dropped open as she watched the witch's mug refill itself with beer, and mead, and wine. Her eyes widened as the witch's dinner plate filled up with piles of chicken, then pork, then beef, then fish. Lissa thought there was enough there to quench the thirst and hunger of an entire army. She pushed her fist into her belly to stop it from rumbling.

The Baba Witch slurped, chewed, and swallowed everything down until she finished her meal with a large belch. Lissa ran across the floor and sat

10

by the fire just as the Baba Witch appeared with a small plate of potatoes. She tossed the bowl at Lissa's feet.

'Eat,' said the witch, and flopped down into her favourite armchair.

Once the witch began to snore, Lissa ate a little of the potato and stuffed the major share of it into her skirt pocket. Then, she too curled up in front of the hearth and enjoyed the heat on her back for another night.

***

When the Baba Witch came home the next night, she found that Lissa had performed every single task that had been assigned to her. With her stomach grumbling from the lack of children's flesh, the Baba Witch stormed up and down the living room raging at Lissa.

'How is it that you, an uneducated village girl, can complete the most exhausting of tasks and still be this pleasant when I come home?'

'Well, Auntie,' said Lissa, 'I am blessed…'

The Baba Witch stopped pacing and cocked her head.

'Blessed?' said the witch. 'What do you mean?'

'Well, when my mother lay dying, I visited her and she…'

'Your mother?'

'Yes, Auntie. She was a very kind and loving person.'

The Baba Witch refused to hear any more.

'Get out. Get out. Get out of my house,' shrieked the old witch.

She pushed Lissa out of the front door and shoved her through the courtyard up to the thorned gate.

'How dare you despoil this place with your blessings,' shouted the Baba Witch. 'If I ever see your spoiled face again…I will eat it!'

'But, Auntie,' pleaded Lissa, 'what about the candles? I cannot return to my stepmother…'

The Baba Witch opened the thorned gate with a chant and shoved Lissa to the ground. Lissa raised her arm to protect herself. But instead of kicking her, the witch pulled a skull out from the fencepost and tossed it at Lissa's feet.

'Take it,' said the Baba Witch, shaking with rage.

'Thank you, Auntie,' whispered Lissa.

'That I may be, but your stepmother knew who she was really sending you to…'

'But stepmother said…'

'Be careful of people who want to tear you down, girl. Now, follow the thin path to the left and you will reach the village before the white and red horses ride out.'

Weeping, Lissa grabbed the skull and stumbled into the forest without looking back. Although she did not feel a tug at her shirt pocket, she was sure the little doll was still in there. Thinking through what she should do next, Lissa held up the human skull and allowed its blue eyes to light her path home.

***

Lissa reached the village as the cockerels began to crow. The main street was empty. Most of the front curtains were drawn and the gas lamps were still lit. When Lissa arrived at her father's townhouse, she was about to open the garden gate and enter through the back door as normal. However, today she decided she had been through enough. Instead of entering through the back door like a servant, she would enter from the main street, just like her stepsisters.

Lissa's stepmother almost choked when she saw Lissa standing on the doorstep alive and full of confidence.

'Hello, Stepmother,' said Lissa with a bold smile she had copied from the Baba Witch. 'Are you surprised to see me?'

Lissa's stepmother stuttered as her two plump daughters came trotting into the hall.

'Hello, Stepsisters,' said Lissa and kicked off her muddy boots. She flung them into a corner and said, 'I am sorry, but the Baba Witch did not eat me.'

'Did…did you get the candles?' asked the youngest stepsister, afraid to look up.

'Oh, I got something better than that,' said Lissa and she held up the skull the Baba Witch had given her.

A shot of blue flame leapt out from the skull's eyes and set fire to her stepsisters until they were two piles of ashes on the floor tiles. Lissa turned to her stepmother next. She held up the skull once more and her stepmother screamed in agony as the blue flames dissolved every last piece of her. Now, there were three piles of grey ashes on the floor.

Lissa was free. She opened her shirt pocket to tell the cloth doll everything she had done, proud of herself for fighting back against her bullies. But, her pocket was empty.

'Dollet?' cried Lissa. 'Dollet, where are you?'

Lissa retraced her steps, knocking over the ashes as she paced up and down shouting for her friend. 'Dollet?' she cried again.

This was the first time that Lissa had not received a reply from the cloth doll. It was lost. Maybe it had fallen out in the forest. Maybe the Baba Witch had taken it. It did not matter now because Lissa could never go back, not without being killed and eaten.

Lissa sat on the stairs and wept. She cried for her mother and for the father who had deserted her long ago. She wept for her little cloth friend and, finally, she wept for herself. After a while, she thought about what the little doll would have said if it was still there in her shirt pocket.

'Don't just sit there crying…do something,' she imagined the cloth doll scolding her.

Lissa took a deep breath and stood up. She had so much to do. She could marry, or find work, or attend school, or even travel the world. It felt good to have so many options. Although Lissa wished with all her heart that Dollet was still there to enjoy it with her, she knew it was time for her to keep her own counsel.

'It was lost. Maybe it had fallen out in the forest. Maybe the Baba Witch had taken it.'

ABOUT THIS TALE

This story was inspired by the work of the Russian folklorist Alexander Afanasyev (1826-1871). Specifically, it follows the structure of *Vasilissa The Fair* where a young girl escapes from a forest-dwelling Baba Yaga. A Baba Yaga was an elderly witch who flew in a mortar and pestle and lived in a hut that walked on chicken feet.

In the Russian folk tales, a Baba Yaga is the embodiment of a powerful nature goddess who harnesses planetary elements. She can either help or harm those who disturb her.

Generation after generation, people have told and re-told popular tales from their part of the world and beyond. Each time, a little something is added to the mix as the teller mines what Salman Rushdie referred to as *'the ocean of story'*. They might add a different plot line here, embellish the character's personality there, or maybe even add an extra layer of motivation to the mix.

As home to a rare species of fungus beetle, and as a Site of Special Scientific Interest, Dundonald Woods became the perfect hunting ground for retelling a Baba Yaga tale. The ruins of Parkthorn House also made an interesting house for her since there is a lot of noise there at certain times of the day and the ground shakes when you approach it.

You can follow Lissa's route through Dundonald Woods by following the path from the Castle Visitor Centre. Once you cross the burn, follow the top right trail. This circular route will bring you past Parkthorn House and return you to the village via Auchans House, the site of our final story.

AE FOND KISS

Robert Kirk, *The Secret Commonwealth of Elves,*
Fauns, and Fairies (1691)

walked to the well again at dusk while the bairn screeched, scarlet-faced and writhing, in its crib. No amount of milk or meat would nourish it. No lullabies could tame it. Drained of my spirits, I chose to leave, even though we had water enough for the following day.

My sighs echoed into the deep black of the well. I sat numb on the cold stone wondering how that angry creature in my home could be the same child who had slid from my womb a few months ago. No words left my lips. The torture was confined to my own head, though my judgement was swift. Whatever lay in that crib did not belong there. Those green eyes, that terrible scowl, this was not my child. If my husband still walked the earth, he'd make sure the owner took it back.

The thought had no sooner slipped away than the air around me grew troubled. Dust spiraled around my feet. My hair extended and danced in all directions. I felt a soft breeze kiss at my neck. It sang in my ear, urging me to let go of my sorrows.

Come with us, it called.

The breeze traced along my throat, down to the swell of my bosom.

Come, it sighed.

The smell of gorse and wild garlic ebbed into the twilight.

Come...

I stretched out my neck and offered myself up to it.

Come...

For those few minutes, I forgot what waited for me at home. The tears. The drudgery. The expectations to remarry.

As soon as these thoughts flowed from me, everything became still, as if nothing had ever happened.

There was a rustle in the trees leading to Kemp Law ridge. I looked up to find hares, roe deer, and a vixen charging up the hill to lay at the feet of a woman. No longer formless, the Queen of the Fane gripped a hunting spear that had a small stone cutting blade bound to its shaft. Curved, white antlers blossomed from the top of her head, her white hair plaited around them like ivy. She wore a string of white cowrie shells around her neck. Her naked body was as firm and as toned as any male warrior's.

The moment our eyes met, we were bonded. She to me and me to her. There was no fear. Just a quivering excitement in my belly, like the one I had on the day I married my husband. Only, this time, the joy was stronger.

The enchantment was soon broken when my nearest neighbour, a local elder, trampled through the forest, crushing twigs and flowers underfoot. My new love vanished with her hunting party then, taking with her the last of the daylight.

'Mistress Hunter,' the elder grumbled, as night descended. 'For what purpose are you out here so late, and bareheaded as well?'

How much the landowner, a man of much self-importance, had witnessed, it was difficult to tell.

Hoping I did not appear as flustered as I felt, I said, 'Yes, Elder. I must hurry back for the bairn.'

'Indeed,' he said, his dark red brows scrunched with concern. There was a trace of ale on his breath. 'But are you not forgetting something?'

'No, I have everything...'

I was about to make for the path back to my cottage when the elder grabbed my shoulder.

'Mistress Hunter,' he said, looking at me askance, his pursed lips dwarfed by his dense, dark red beard. 'Were you not here to make use of the well?'

'Oh,' I said. 'I must have been mistaken...we have water already...'

I smiled and fixed my hair as he checked me over, but my cheeks flushed at the memory of the Queen's soft kisses.

'Is that so?' said the elder, letting go of me. 'Then I bid you a good evening.'

As soon as he strode away, I knew I had not been well received. My neighbour would accuse me of indecency, I was sure of it. Like Eve, I would be marked as a fallen woman.

A small bird flitted out from the branches as I stumbled home.

***

I was forced to appear at the Kirk Session on the following Thursday. They prosecuted me first before attending to the Sabbath breaker and the beggar.

'Session held on this fifteenth day of Julii, 1602,' announced the Minister. 'Presenting thereat James Wallace, heritor and elder, Thomas Wallace of Gullilandis, Patrick Bryding of Holmes, and John Forgushill, younger of Halie, deacons.'

The Minister cleared his throat.

'Now, you, Janet Hunter,' he said to me, his eyes wild and full of damnation, 'you have been compelled to appear before this Session to answer to the charge of fornication…how plead you?'

My mouth opened and closed, unable to form words. Shocked murmurs trickled around the cramped and stuffy hall.

'Do you deny it then?' shouted James Wallace, my neighbour, rising from his chair beside the other dignitaries. He shook his fist. 'Would you deny, here in the presence of God, that I found you in the hanging woods that night, red-faced and without your bonnet?'

What could I say? If I confessed to fornication with a nature goddess, I would be burned as a witch. So, I nodded. When they demanded to know the name of my bedfellow, I shook my head. When I saw the child crying and kicking in the arms of the elder's wife, I said nothing. No pangs struck my full and heavy bosom at its distress. No traces of milk ran down the inside of my shift. What further proof did I need?

Mistress Wallace is not holding my bairn, I thought. *That is not my son, but I will find him, if I keep my faith.*

The trial continued around me with the Session pronouncing my guilt.

'As a confirmed fornicatrix,' cried the Minister, 'you are hereby ordained to pay XX shillings unlaw…'

'No,' I cried. 'How can I?'

'Or,' continued the Minister, 'you shall abide in the castle of Dundonald for three days imprisonment and thereafter to stand several Sundays, in sackcloth, barefooted and bareheaded, at the Kirk end…'

The room mumbled their agreement at my sentence.

'…and there you will stand,' said the Minister, 'from the ringing of the first bell until the very last, in the place of repentance until the preaching and the prayers be completed…'

Mistress Wallace, the elder's wife, held up the bairn to me, mouthing heartfelt promises to keep it safe for me until I returned to the fold. For the sake of appearances, I thanked her for her God-given generosity.

Although that is not my son you're cradling, I smiled to myself.

Before they dragged me through the village to the castle dungeon, I saw the same small bird from the forest the other night. It perched on the Kirk roof and watched me spit at the elder's feet. It flew away again before he drew his sword.

***

If I had been born of a more blessed stock, they might have gifted me the small room above the dungeon pit to see out my punishment. There, at least, was a small fireplace and room enough to walk upright to relieve an aching back. There was even a small window to chart the sunrise and a latrine.

However, I am not so blessed, and there were none of these things in the pit. Chained in the darkness, my skin prickled whenever the spiders, creatures the size of bannocks, danced across it. My swollen breasts were almost dry and were hot to the touch. I knocked the left one when I kicked away a rat and the pain caused me to weep.

Early on the Sabbath, just an hour before my release, I felt a soft breeze graze my cheek. Having cried myself hoarse through the night, and with a cold sweat laying on my brow, I was sure I felt the Queen's soft kisses. At first, I thought it was delirium, but then the light fragrance of gorse and wild garlic flowed into the darkness.

Will you come with us now? sang the Queen.

'What about my son?' I insisted. 'I must get to him…he will be hungry and tired, and missing me sorely.'

He is well taken care of.

'But that creature Mistress Wallace is nursing is not mine.'

No, but perhaps your son is already with us. Why not let Mistress Wallace keep the changeling?

The Queen caressed my forehead with her cool, soft kisses.

'But my own son is well?' I asked, trying to raise myself up.

Hush, sang the Queen. *you will need your energy for dancing. In the land of the Fane you will drink the sweetest nectar and feast on the ripest berries. There will be flutes and games and careless days spent chasing the sun and hunting the moon. All this will come to pass, if you join us of your own will.*

'But my son?' I insisted. 'Prove to me you have him first…'

As the Queen's caresses intensified, I felt the heat of summer on my face. In my mind, I was laying, not on soiled, moss-covered stone, but on lush grass surrounded by blossoming trees. I was eating soft fruits and watching my black-haired son pick wildflowers for my hair.

'Chained in the darkness, my skin prickled whenever the spiders,
creatures the size of bannocks, danced across it.'

I couldn't picture my husband, for he must have lost faith in the Fane, but I saw my boy clearly. Before I could question the Queen further, the door to the pit slid open and she was gone. The rush of fresh air and light assaulted my senses. My belly started to heave.

'Time for your penance, Mistress Hunter,' said the young guard climbing down to get me.

He removed my chains, but since my legs could not tolerate standing, he was forced to carry me back up. He complained loudly as he did so.

'Put this on,' the guard grumbled when we returned to the surface. He threw the rough sackcloth at me and said, 'And you'd better be quick about it because Wallace the Elder will be along shortly to shave your head before you enter the Kirk.'

***

My neighbour, James Wallace, dug his nails into my throat while he robbed me of my feminine looks. As he snipped and hacked and pulled at my hair, he tried to provoke my passions by castigating me with harsh words. I refused to give him the satisfaction of tears and anger. All I thought about was running carefree in the hanging wood with my son.

There was nothing the elder could do now to hurt me. So, let my tresses fall. If the Queen proves my son is with her, I will gladly be gone from this world.

***

The sun was out, but still I shivered. My shorn head, patchy in a few places, allowed me to experience an extra layer of cold I'd never felt before. Although my fever was still advancing, I knew I would stand on the wooden cutty stool, rather than sit on it. What did I care about wearing the scratchy, used sackcloth, or that my naked feet were plastered with mud and faeces from trudging up the main street?

The three-legged stool wobbled on the Kirk floor, but I still had hope that the Queen would come. Unlike my husband, I would try to keep my faith. This certainty gave me the courage to meet every eye of every neighbour who tried to judge me with their scrunched lips and pious head shaking. The Minister tried his best to make me shame-faced from his pulpit.

'And so sayeth Saint Paul in his first letter to the Corinthians, "Neither let us commit fornication, as some of them committed fornication, and fell, in one day..."' the Minister shouted, banging his fist to punctuate his scripture, "three and twenty thousand..."'

The seconds and minutes ticked away as the Minister riled up the congregation. Then an hour passed with no answer from the Queen. Had I been wrong? When Mistress Wallace, the elder's wife, held up the bairn to me, as if to show me what I still had to live for, I could not laugh at her. I tried to, but the urge soon dissipated. What if that small, unhappy creature she held really was my son? My heart drummed in time with the Minister's pounding fist. If I could just keep my faith...

But soon I could take no more of the waiting. In a fit of defiance, I shouted at the elder's wife, 'That is not mine, I tell you. That bairn is not of my womb and it is not of this world...'

Mistress Wallace covered the bairn's ears and shrieked. A commotion spread around the Kirk, causing the purple-faced Minister to roar for calm and restraint. Even though my bosom ached, and I still poured with sweat, I could not stop myself from fighting back. What a peculiar spectacle I must have made, and yet how strange they all were. A whole village of people pointing and judging me when they all had their own sins to hide.

'And you James Wallace, elder of this parish,' I shouted with my hands outstretched. 'My own neighbour...why ever were you in the hanging wood that night?'

James Wallace spluttered and rose to his feet cursing my name and my lineage. The men around him held him back by his shoulders, counselling him to show mercy as my soul was clearly troubled.

'Your breeches were unfastened,' I cackled. 'What had you been up to? Were you merely emptying your bladder, as you claimed, or was it something more shameful? The beard on your face is as red and as overgrown as the one in your breeches after all...'

There was shock and uproar throughout the Kirk. The Minister raged. I didn't care because the little bird from before had returned. It roosted on the pulpit, holding a lock of fine, black hair in its beak. My Queen had sent proof after all. My son was with her. I could leave now.

In the midst of the congregation's chattering, a cool breeze danced around me. There was a hint of gorse and wild garlic as it kissed along my neck.

Will you come with us now? the Queen of the Fane whispered in my ear.

'Yes,' I wept with relief, 'I will.'

As she brushed away my tears with a last fond kiss, I took a final breath. I had kept my faith. My reward was to join my son in the eternal hunt where we would feast and drink and dance forever.

Back amongst the congregation, horrified mouths fell open as my fevered body fell limp to the Kirk floor. Women wailed, men squawked, and the tongue-tied Minister finally fell silent.

When they saw the little bird flying away from the building, they later claimed it was my broken soul leaving to make peace with its Maker. The truth was lost on them.

But what does that matter? They can keep my old bones.

ABOUT THIS TALE

'Ae fond kiss, and then we sever!
Ae fareweel alas, for ever!'

Robert Burns, *Ae Fond Kiss* (1791)

This story was inspired by entries in the Dundonald Kirk Session records from the early 1600s. Alongside adulterers, fornicators, and sabbath breakers, people like Marion Or confessed to going *'thruch the parochin professing hir self to ryd with the fair folk.'*

From the fifteenth to the nineteenth centuries, fairy belief in Scotland was prevalent across society. In folklore, charms incorporating iron were used for protection against these malevolent, human-sized supernatural beings. Fairies were often believed to kill livestock and to kidnap human children.

Referred to by euphemisms like the Fair Folk, or the Fane in Ayrshire, fairies were linked to Neolithic burial mounds and Iron Age brochs and duns, like the one at Kemp Law by Dundonald's Smuggler's Trail. They were also associated with the souls of the dead.

However, fairy belief was inextricably linked with witchcraft. In 1597, King James VI wrote in his Daemonologie that fairies were the result of the Devil *'ravishing'* the imagination of witches to bewitch them into thinking they were entering *'such glistering courts and traines'* of the fairies. To him, fairies were demons and those who believed in them were a threat to Christian society.

Local Presbyterian Kirk Sessions policed morality in their parishes and also meted out punishments. In Dundonald, fornicators received fines and public penance. Some were incarcerated in the castle. It should be noted that 'notorious' adultery was outside the Kirk Session's mandate as it was made a capital offence in 1563.

The real-life Janet Hunter was tried and executed for witchcraft in 1604, when the Dundonald Kirk Session included the minister, David Mylne. Her prosecutor, James Wallace, was also the Baillie of Kyle and the local prosecutor in the next story.

DEVIL OF LOUDOUN HILL

The Pain and the Panic

ondemned, and soon to have his flesh burnt to ashes, Patrick Lowrie feels the executioner's fingers tighten around his throat. Memories come in flashes. He can't remember if all he has said before the Kirk Session is true or if it is a devilish mirage.

At the burning site on Edinburgh's castle hill, Lowrie's heart is ready to burst. He tries twisting away from the meaty hands enveloping him. All the small man can do is yank on his chains and piss his breeches.

The Hunger

Lowrie's lungs ache. He pleads for his ribs to expand. One small gasp should do it. The pressure surges from his chest and discharges into the constriction around his neck. His nostrils burn.

Lowrie's head feels like a swollen pustule about to rupture, as if his brain is about to explode over the thronging street.

The fight for existence drains his energy fast. He grows limp. His dark fringe slumps over his face. The two blue orbs of his eyes burn as if they are being boiled in oil.

A memory flutters in the approaching blackness.

Before the trial, seventy-six miles away, back home in Dundonald, the old men instruct the young men to walk Lowrie in circles. His feet are bare and blistered. Each time sleep threatens to release him, they tour his body around the icy room.

- But I'm hungry, says Lowrie.
- Food is for the weak, the young men mock him.

- Let me sleep, Lowrie begs.
- But sleep is for the guilty, the old men scold him.

How long does this last? Weeks? Hours? At this point, trying to hold onto time is like snatching at sand. Another flash of memory.
- Why did you refuse to plough your field at Beltane, Patrick?
- I had business elsewhere.
- You were not adhering to some notorious pagan custom then?
- No.
Lowrie cries out. The men rage at his rambling, unsatisfactory answers. The bodkin pins hurt his flesh and the mole in his armpit does not bleed. It's a sign.

The White Light

The executioner releases his fingers a little to toy with Lowrie's breath and then cuts the air off for the final time. Although the capital is overcast, a searing white light tears through Lowrie's mind. Conscious, albeit briefly, he shakes his chains with all the fury he can muster. They hardly move.

What does *maleficium* mean? The Kirk Session says he dug up corpses.
- Did he do it?
- He must have.
- Did he dismember the dead?
- If they say he did.
- In a ritual?
- Yes.
- Alone?
- Yes…no.
- Accomplices?
- Women. Neighbours.
- How many?
- Three.
- From where?
- Halie.
- Where?
- Highlees farmtoun, on the hill track between Dundonald and Loans.

The Ringing in the Ears

Lowrie smells the executioner's sweat and the reek of his own soiled breeches. The faces in the crowd blur. Their shouts dissolve. Pressure builds. Something pops. Eardrums? A vein?

Another flash. Lowrie's grey-haired minister is testifying as an expert witness. The same man who blessed his parents' union, and performed his baptism, shakes his head at him from across the court.

'Oh, aye,' the minister tells the Justice-depute whilst twisting his pious hands. 'Patrick Lowrie is a noted witch. In fact, it is weel kent throughout the village that the man is cursed by the Deil, like his ain faither was...'

Vomit in the Lungs

The contents of Lowrie's stomach, unable to break free in the usual way, jettison into his lungs. He feels as though he is standing at the bottom of the ocean, leagues below the reach of the sun.

Lowrie's brain flares. Memories are less concrete now. One moment he's tied to the stake in Edinburgh. In the next, his spirit is flying over Loudoun Hill.

At the grey volcanic stack, back home in Ayrshire, the Hallowe'en night is moonless. A bonfire crackles on the hilltop throwing shadows over the naked flesh gyrating in front of it.

Is this really happening? It must be. He can smell suckling pig and taste blood in his mouth.

Maggie Duncan, Katherine McTeir, and the long-dead Janet Hunter dance in circles around him. Lowrie's mouth moves and he sings along with the women until a dark shadow glides towards them. The diabolical presence offers Lowrie a large pelt of brown hair. He obliges and takes it. The pelt has five sharpened claws at the end; four fingers and one twisted thumb. The shadow flickers. First, it has horns. Then, none.

The devil walks among them, or so says the confession he put his mark to.

The Voicebox Crushed

Lowrie's larynx breaks beneath the executioner's grip. Lowrie screams inside his head.

He remembers the roots of his injustice.

- Why do you allow this man to prosecute me? Lowrie shouts at the Kirk Session elders. How can this same corrupt man, the Baillie of Kyle, the one who tried to take my land, how can he ensure me a fair trial?

Finding Peace

Lowrie's final sparks of life. He sees the fertile rolling hills of Halie. Clear, bright skies. Sheep grazing on the outfield. Loudoun Hill in the distance.

Lowrie is back behind the plough, wiping his soaking forehead. Although this poor, rocky land is usually left untouched as the Devil's portion, Lowrie needs to expand his crop this year.

- You mustn't plough the Gudeman's Croft, she says, shaking her head.
- Bellies must still be filled in winter, says Lowrie, forcing his horse on.
- But the Deil will come for ye, Pat, she says. He'll come for ye...
- Be gone with your ungodly superstition, he laughs at her.

Now, as the executioner lights the torches, Lowrie curses himself for not listening. If he had only heard the wise woman out, then maybe...maybe.

As the executioner lights the piled-up faggots beneath Lowrie's chained feet, the soles of the farmer's shoes start to melt. Whatever dregs of life are left in Lowrie are soon extinguished by the woodsmoke.

He is the first of many devils to be disposed of this day.

'Lowrie's final sparks of life. He sees the fertile rolling hills of Halie. Clear, bright skies. Sheep grazing on the outfield. Loudoun Hill in the distance.'

ABOUT THIS TALE

Although men like Patrick Lowrie were executed for witchcraft, it was mostly women who bore the brunt of the Scottish witch hunts between 1563 and 1736. According to The Survey of Scottish Witchcraft, of the 3,212 known accused, about 86% were female.

In disputes regarding suspected witchcraft, the accused and the accuser were normally of equal social status. The most common suspect was between the ages of 50 and 60 and was well-known in the community, usually married to, or a widow of, a middle-class peasant or tradesman.

While neighbours might complain of magical harm being done to their person or livestock, it was at the ministerial and judiciary level where the accusation of a demonic pact was introduced. Although judicial torture was legal, it was illegal at Kirk Session level. However, this did not prevent the Kirk Session from using tactics like sleep deprivation to encourage a confession.

Over the space of half a decade, Patrick Lowrie went from being accused of deliberately not ploughing his fields at Beltane, considered a pagan tradition in post-Reformation Scotland, to being on trial in Edinburgh for witchcraft. He was executed in 1604.

Alongside Janet Hunter, Katherine McTeir, and Margaret Duncan, Lowrie was accused of folk healing and bewitching cattle as well as more serious crimes. These included dismembering corpses in magical rituals and the holding of witch sabbats. Subsequently, Lowrie confessed to meeting the Devil in the form of a woman named Helena McBurnie on Loudoun Hill on Hallowe'en night. McBurnie was said to have presented the 'witches' with a hair pelt in the shape of the Devil's claws.

AIT THE SMUGGLER'S GRAVE

he first tae blame is Alexander Gordon, the surveyor o customs. Postit alang the coast ait Ayr, he wis a poker-backit, craw-beakit type o man intent on provin himsel.

He's no noo, mind ye. Like me, he's nae mair than auld banes dressit up in raggedy claes an loupin wi wirms. Bit, in they days, he wis a despicable, upstaunin sort wha niver cuid turn a blin ee.

He wid prod his informers tae haunt us - haunt us - fae yin muin tae anither, oniethin tae stoap oor wherries landin goods at the Troon. They intendit tae rob us o oor profits, an we intendit tae mak shair the royal poakets stayed licht.

Aye, smugglers.

Ken hoo monie o this village were involved? Men - an women - fae aw across the parish. Guid, hardy sorts fae families we trustit. Ye needit several hunner pairs o hauns tae shift they loads.

Although A went oan tae dabble in hogsheads o tobacco an bushels o tea, the Loans Company was aw aboot the rum in 1766. Wi hard rain stoatin aff oor cheeks, an oor fingers numb wi the cauld, we cairrit the heavy widden casks bi lantern licht. Fae the boats tae the cairts. Fae the boats tae horseback. Nae maitter the weather, we liftit an we stackit ait speed, less Alexander Gordon's spies breengit upon us in the derk.

Some o the Company came airmed wi pistols. Ithers came wi sticks tae fecht thaim aff. Passions were high, ye see, ever since the King stole the Isle of Man trade fir hissel. 'Cause o him, oor operations needit tae shift tae Ireland, an that cost us a lot o coin.

Bit, bi then, tenants were keen tae clipe oan their landlords. Even cairters, an coopers, an smiddies, an innkeepers, an the like, felt the need tae unburden thaimsels aboot their neeboors. All fir the need o the King's siller. It wis a sad time, an no like the glory days afore it.

Sae relations atween the likes o us Dundonald fowk an the Ayr excisemen grew fraught. If onie o Gordon's men turned up on oor coast… weel, let's jist say they goat given mair than the evil een.

In deith, A dae miss the rummel o the tide an the reek o kelp rottin oan the sands. A remember five hunner impatient cuddies snortin, aw strainin at the bit fir tae get their loads shiftit. A remember the village fowk sweatin through a thoosand weary steps tae cairy casks back an forrit. A cuid niver forget the thrum o thair weel-kent voices in the derk.

This wan nicht there wis a shadowy figure sittin oan horseback oan the ither side o the dunes. Davie Dunlop, the heid man o the Loans Company, keekit him first. Big Davie gied a whistle fir me tae tak a keek anaw. Richt awa, A kent this stranger wis a spy sent bi the surveyor o customs, Alexander Gordon. Yon meant airmit dragoons wir no lang ahint him.

A gied Davie the nod fir there wis much fir us aw tae lose. If we hid a been caught oot there wi aw that cargo, oor futures - an scores o lives - wid hiv been in ruins. Havin His Majesty's Coort in Edinburgh fine us treble the value o the rum wid hae bankruptit the entire Loans Company. Nae wey onie o us cuid cough up £6,000.

Sae three o Davie's hard men creepit oot tae challenge the intruder. They grabbit his coat an tore him fae his mount, sendin his hat birlin intae the dirt. They grabbit his stick an his pistols, an then they bruisit him sarely. Fist efter fist. Kick efter kick.

Then, spittin an swearin, they roarit oot, 'Return wance mair an ye'll forfeit yer life…'

The customs officer's face was aw bloody an smasht like a hauf-chowit neep. Bit - an this still maks me keel ower wi laughter - bi the time the King's men arryvit ait the Troon shore, fu o passion, they were sarely disappointit tae fin aw the evidence hid been spiritit awa…nae muskets saw action yon nicht.

Shortly efter, mind, twa writs were gied tae ma wife Annie, in front o ma weans. A wis away fae Holms fairm, ye see. Ma bonnie Annie was awfu bad wi her nerves. Since her servant pal wis awa oot ait the apothecary, Annie hid tae tak receipt o the writs hersel. She was much distressit when A set fit back in the hoose.

'Edinburgh, Matthew,' she wept. 'Ye've tae gang tae coort in Edinburgh.'

A telt her no tae boather aboot the likes o Alexander Gordon, that we'd suin see him aff, bit Annie wrung her haunds through tae the morn, scratchin her skin raw wi the wirry.

Oan anither black nicht like this yin, Alexander Gordon wis headin hame tae Ayr. Comin fae Irvine, he wis accompanit bi a local merchant ca'ed McMurtrie.

Wrappit in ma heavy overcoat, an wi ma tricorn pu'd doon low, A rode past thaim ait great speed, as if perchance A wis bound fir Ayr tae on a grave an urgent maitter. Bit ait the final moment, A jabbit ma mount's sides an A stormit aff the nairra track. Hidin in the bushes, fower o Big Davie's servants were awaitin ma signal, ready fir tae dae Gordon ill oan ma command.

'It is him,' A cried. 'Mak ready…'

An as the unwittin hooves approchit, A gave the order. The gunpouther explodit as ilka servant fyrit upon Gordon. Hooever, Gordon's cuddy, anticipatin the danger, jerkit awa. The bullets didnae reach their terget. McMurtrie's mount rose up insteid an bore the woonds intendit fir Alexander Gordon. McMurtrie wis tippit ontae his fat rump, leavin Gordon untroublit.

Suin efter, the authorities stairtit questionin the hale o Dundonald parish aboot the affair. There must hiv been a squeal aboot 'cause A wis merchit aff tae the tolbooth in Ayr an chairgit wi attemptit murder. There A wis held withoot bail. Puir, hairt-sick Annie cuidnae see me. A even scrievit her a letter hopin her servant wid read it oot tae her. A niver heard back.

Bit A wisnae to waste awa on breid an watter like some unfortunate creatures did. Ma monie companions deliverit me ale an entertainments, an we ate, drank, an makit merry till A wis freed. A even played a gemme or twa o chess.

In the end, whit proof o ma guilt did Alexander Gordon hiv? Davie's men hid lang since boardit *The Unicorn* fir France, an Gordon's unfortunate travellin companion, McMurtrie, hid fled intae the mirk. Sae, it turns oot Ah'm nae murderer efter aw, which maks ma tale aw the sorrier.

Ach, noo, the Kirk bells are ringin midnicht as we speir. A hae less than a meenit afore the Beast comes tearin ait ma sowel. Sae afore he drags me back tae his fiery pit, A will get tae the hairt o the maitter. Since yer sat here oan ma grave, Ah'll tell ye.

The second tae blame is Elizabeth Wilson. It wis she wha stirred the arsenic intae her kin's denner. Ah'm shair o it. When A came callin ait the hoose yon day, she wis wirkin the sowens bi the fire, steepin the oat husks in the hoat watter. Her breists were gey heavy lukkin, an her belly wis swollen bi a few months, A cuid tell. Bit her deif stepmither, auld Betty, she wis spinnin wool beside her an she wis oblivious tae it aw, as wis her faither.

A usually went tae Plewlands fir tae supervise the ploughin, bit when her stepmither, the auld skinny nag, hid steppit oot o the front room, A ran ower tae Elizabeth tae let oan ma real reason fir bein there.

'We shud speir aboot ye gang aff tae Edinburgh afore it's yer tyme tae gie birth,' A said.

'Since yer sat here oan ma grave, Ah'll tell ye...'

Aye, A confess it. A wantit Elizabeth oot the wey afore the news o ma adultery reached Annie. If ma puir wife hid foond oot aboot Elizabeth's bairn… nae boady else kent it wis mine then, ye see.

Next thing, A hears auld Betty his spewit hersel tae deith an Elizabeth's faither the verra same. Bi aw accoonts, they writhed fir several days afore they passit ower. Elizabeth's sister wis sae ill that she niver yaised her legs agin fir the rest o her life. Even the puir fairm cat sufferit.

The only yin wha didnae feel the torment o the poison wis Elizabeth hersel. Och, bit she ate the sowens fu o arsenic, didn't she? Aye, bit she hid the guid fortune tae vomit it back up straight awa…lucky fir her, eh? Wrang. It wisnae luck.

Bit the dragoons came fir me agin, didn't they? 'Cause A said A wis the wean's faither, didn't A? Even though Ah'm gey shair Elizabeth Wilson bedded ithers afore me, the wikkit harlot that she wis. An 'cause A wis in the howf at Plewlands yon day, Lord Kames thocht A hid the opportunity tae slip arsenic intae the sowens… me bein a fairmer an aw, yaisin arsenic tae kill the rats…Weel, guess wha wis chairgit wi murder an sentencit fir tae hang ait Ayr?

Aye, me. Me wi yon thick rope aroon his neck. Me wha niver hurt onieboady…me. Nae her. Nae Elizabeth Wilson, the yin wha wantit tae stoap her kin fae finin oot aboot her sins.

Ma sweet Annie foond oot aboot it bi the end. Her servant tried her best to keep it fae her o coorse…bit ither tongues in the village waggit happily.

There wis nineteen - nineteen - stairs fae the tollbooth cell tae the tap o the gallows. It tuik wan second tae drap. See oniethin wrang wi ma neck? It's no thrawn, is it? Ah'm hale. Ma spine didnae snap. It means A wis starvit o air fir mair thin ten meenits. The torture lastit 'til ma lungs an ma hairt gied oot…then came the angel lust.

Forgie ma laughter here, bit A promised masel A wid mak this richt. Och, bit it's no revenge Ah'm efter. Alexander Gordon and Elizabeth Wilson are baith lang deid. Naw, if Ah'm tae taste the constant horrors o Hell, A wid want tae be hung fir a sheep as well as fir a lamb…

Whit dae ye think A mean?

That's it. Keep oan runnin. Ah'll watch as ye try tae push through the iron gates o the graveyard. Bit see hoo A swing thaim shut afore ye kin get there. Aye, bi aw means check the locks. Rattle the gates, if ye must. Or, ye kin try tae climb ower the iron spikes, if ye dare. Pu ower the heidstanes as ye run awa tae. That's it. Tummel the stane urn tae the groond. It willnae slow me doon… Or ye kin dae as yer daein noo, an crawl backwards 'til ye slam against the rough trunk o yon sycamore. Ye'll niver climb up it fast eneuch afore A get tae ye. There's nae wey oot. That's it, bawl yer lungs oot.

The inn is lang closit. Naeboady decent is up an aboot at this tyme o nicht. Yer waistin yer breath. Yer tyme's up.

Eh? Whit dae ye think A want?

A wid ken whit it is like tae actually tak a life. A wid haud ma finger banes aroon yer neck an throttle ye, jist tae see hoo it feels. A wid see yer een bulge an yer tongue swell, an yer bowels empty. A wid feel yer hairt stoap. A wid be mair than satisfied wi yon.

Sae quieten doon. A will hae justice.

'That's it. Tummel the stane urn tae the groond. It willnae slow me doon...'

A BOOT THIS TALE

This story is based on the extensive research carried out by Dr Frances Wilkins into the Loans Smugglers and the life of the smuggler Matthew Hay of Holms, Gailes, and Plewlands farms. Although David Dunlop, the head of the Loans Company, and Matthew Hay are both buried in Dundonald churchyard, only David Dunlop's headstone remains.

While in Ayr Tolbooth, awaiting trial for the murder of his tenants, Hay writes to his wife Ann's attendant, Peggy Dunlop. While he protests his innocence in these letters, he also shows remorse for his sexual impropriety and begs Peggy not to tell Ann he is the father of Elizabeth Wilson's baby.

Hay writes these letters in formal English, but the writer likes to think he may have spoken Ayrshire Scots in person.

Matthew Hay's trial started at 7am on Friday 8th September 1780 and lasted until the same time the next day. It was presided over by judge Lord Kames who was a chess playing friend of Hay's. Although Hay maintained his innocence, contemporary accounts in the Scots Magazine say that '*the jury returned their verdict finding, by a great plurality of voices, the pannel Guilty.*'

There are reports that when Lord Kames was about to leave court, he leant over to Hay's Advocate and said, '*There's checkmate to you, Matthew.*'

Matthew Hay was hanged at Ayr on Friday 13th October 1780. As dictated at his sentencing, his body was delivered to a surgeon in Ayr for dissection and all his property was taken by the Crown.

While Hay did try to have the surveyor of customs murdered, Dr Wilkins argues he might be innocent of the murder of his tenants. Then again, he might not be.

THE AUCHANS PEAR

ith a genteel wave of her hand, Lady Susanna Montgomerie bade farewell to her visitors; the well-renowned English Man of Letters, Dr Samuel Johnson, and his companion, James Boswell Esq. Now in her eighty-fifth year, she remembered when visitors to the Auchans dower house in Ayrshire had not been so rare, especially ones of such breeding and intellect.

Alone in the long drawing-room, near a vigorous fire, she thought back to the fancies of her youth. Of candlelit entertainments in the capital, enthusing over the latest scientific advancements. Of lively, often table-thumping, discussions on points of moral philosophy, or on the most recent politics, laughing inwardly at the rising classes who, in the city, tried to mask their fine west coast accents with a more civilised and learned diction. There had been dancing too, as well as poetry and music. All the highest of arts enjoyed in the finest company.

Instead of the widow's wine she was reduced to serving now, there had been unlimited claret and port. Of course, Dr Johnson would have appreciated such refinements, but instead of wincing at the lesser quality libation she had offered, he had remarked on how well it had matched the beef.

'Such a gentleman,' said Lady Susanna with a nod.

She tapped on the oak panelling beside her and opened a secret passageway in the wall. As she did so, a line of *Ratti norvegicus* scuttled onto the desk. There they stood in the glow of the firelight with their long whiskers, pink ears, worm-like tails, and sharp but dainty claws.

'*Bienvenue*. Come bide a while with me, Betty, Susie, Peggie, Fanny, Christie, Ellie,' called Lady Susanna. 'And you likewise, Grace…and darling, James, Alexander, Archie…and little Lotte…'

Lady Susanna took out her handkerchief and unwrapped it, to the delight of her scampering guests. Unbeknownst to the servants, the Countess had smuggled in its contents from the adjoining dining room.

'A fine Auchans Pear for- Oh, Lotte!' cried Lady Susanna. 'Na, na, you wait your turn,' she said, wagging her finger at the smallest guest who had tried to steal the bounty.

Eleven noses twitched as Lady Susanna carved up slices of the winter pear with its lumpy, russet skin still intact.

'A piece for you…and you…and you…' she said, parcelling out the dessert and wrapping up the remains. 'The mother tree was shipped over from France during the time of Queen Mary, God Rest Her…not that I made mention of this to the gentlemen this evening…'

Lady Susanna leaned back in her chair and basked in the thrill of the day.

'I dare tell you that Dr Johnson's sympathies for the Stuart cause are long past,' she told her little guests. 'Imagine the auld Tory's face if I'd shown him the painting in my bedroom? God rest the Old Pretender's troubled soul…'

Pulling herself out of a momentary reverie, she continued, 'But Dr Johnson did so enjoy the pear. "Rich, buttery and juicy," he called it, and so it is, *mes petits*.'

She stroked the soft bellies of her guests while they ate.

'Yes, such a gentleman,' she repeated, 'and our views on religious matters; broadly the same.'

The Dowager Countess smiled to herself. 'By all accounts,' she said, 'he was quite taken with me, and I him.'

She pressed her hand to her bosom.

'And what was that remark of his?'

Lady Susanna imitated the doctor's baritone voice, and with a half-bow, she said, "Dear Lady, you give the laws of Elegance to Scotland".'

At once, her face flushed and her blue eyes, once the colour of summer skies, sparked into life.

'I must confess,' she continued, 'that I am better positioned than most at my time of life. Indeed, Dr Johnson was surprised to learn of a time when I was not so highly prized…'

Finished with their treats, the Countess' guests lost interest in her story and investigated the desktop. They sniffed and peered over the edge as if inspecting the elaborately patterned floor coverings below. All the while, their shadows moved over the corniced ceiling and roamed the painted walls. Eleven sets of tails, ears, teeth, and claws haunted the grand room.

Lady Susanna clapped; two mannerly taps in quick succession upon her palm.

'*Garde-à-Vous*,' she commanded.

On cue, the animals returned to their mistress, ready for her next tale. With some sitting on her lap, a few on the desk, and one large male balanced upon her shoulder, Lady Susanna spoke about her long-dead husband.

'Did you know, my dear ones, that my Lord Montgomerie wished to have me dismissed? Hmm. Back in 1710, in the days when poets still thought my complexion was as soft as the flowers in the walled garden. I was abed with our Betty then, and my Lord had grown quite tired of a succession of daughters. So, he demanded a son or else...divorce.'

The large male on Lady Susanna's shoulder sniffed at her silver hair.

'Indeed, James,' she responded to it. 'So, I said to His Lordship that he was most welcome to do such a thing if, and only if, he could give me back everything that I had brought to the marriage. To which my Lord Montgomerie replied that he was not an unreasonable man and would ensure the swift return of my dowry. Well, my sweet ones, I raised myself up...'

The Countess took on the bearing of her younger self and said, '...and I squared my shoulders and I informed him, "Na, na, my Lord. That will not do. First, return me my youth, my beauty, and my virginity. Then, and only then, can you dismiss me as you wish!"'

Lady Susanna shook her head at the memory. She sighed and returned to her usual, albeit slightly hunched, position. Leaning in close to the guest on her shoulder, she allowed it to nibble the frill of her bonnet.

'But within the year,' she said, smoothing its rough, brown coat against her cheek, 'your namesake was born...my son James, and...Oh...'

Several teeth nipped at the Countess' fingers, looking for the remains of the soft fruit. Reaching again for her handkerchief, she rewarded them with the final slices of pear.

'This last for you...and you,' she said not noticing the little drops of scarlet that now dripped from the teeth marks on her fingers.

With her guests busy, Lady Susanna continued her ruminations on the day's events. '...and dare I say that when I mentioned about my Lord Montgomerie restoring my virginity, Dr Johnson let out such an exclamation that he see-sawed back and forth in his chair. The poor boy, Boswell, couldn't even look up from his shoe buckles...'

Lady Susanna allowed herself a small shriek and copied the esteemed doctor's movements as she relayed the story. Some of her guests absconded in fright at her sudden display. Calming down, the Countess allowed herself a chuckle before her face sank into solemnity.

'Of course, I had quite forgotten young Boswell was acquainted with my son Alexander in boyhood...'

The Countess thought over the last four years since her son's murder at the hands of a local poacher and exciseman.

'Dr Johnson, always the gentleman, remarked upon the travesty of the matter,' said Lady Susanna finishing her thoughts aloud, 'and I do confess that his well-meaning condolences revived my sorrows, rather than lulled them. But, regardless, I replied to him, "Ay, Alexander had both learning and good nature, as well as a natural sweetness of temper that stayed with him into his adult life, cut short though it was by that coward and scoundrel." And Boswell nodded sagely while the esteemed doctor tapped his foot faster and scratched at his wig. Still, I steadied myself and carried on the conversation. Then, I...I...I...I...'

Lady Susanna's attention was lost in the flames of the fire. She toyed with her wedding ring and all at once felt the many wounds that her guests had inflicted on her person. But, how could she blame them for their hunger? Sucking the blood from each of her fingers, the Countess' eyes glazed as she transported herself in time and place, back to another castle, back to her life before Auchans. The side of her mouth twitched as her mind's eye envisioned a pistol crack, a sudden flash of smoke, and a red hole expanding in her child's abdomen.

'So much blood,' she whispered, blinking away her heartache.

However, her little guests had gone their separate paths, oblivious to her distress. They roamed surfaces, knocked over the inkwell, and left a trail behind them. They climbed the heavy drapes and chewed the edges of soft furnishings until there was an apologetic knock on the drawing-room door, followed by polite coughing.

'My Lady Eglinton,' said the maid.

'One moment,' replied the Countess and double-tapped her palm again. '*Arrête pour ce soir*,' she said to her guests, like a schoolmaster herding unruly infants.

Her charges obeyed and, when she slid open the secret passageway in the wood panelling once again, the little guests scampered through it dutifully. There they went into the darkness, as if off to bed.

'*Bonne nuit, mes petits*,' said Lady Susanna blowing a kiss and then replacing the wall panel.

Once she had relocated to the burgundy chaise next to the hearth, and once she had smoothed down her skirts, fixed her bonnet, and tucked her bloodied fingers under her shawl, she allowed the maid to enter.

As the young woman busied herself with the coals and brushed up the animal droppings, Lady Susanna closed her eyes. Having outlived most of her eleven children, and feeling the afflictions of her age, she endeavoured to bear her sufferings with fortitude.

As the pains of her losses began to subside, she took heart in having added one more son to her number. For this evening, just after the final drinks, she had adopted a certain doctor who had grown disagreeable about being born way back in the year 1709.

With the maid gone, Lady Susanna stared at the round-faced putti on the marble mantlepiece and was reminded of the earlier conversation.

'Dr Johnson,' she remembered saying, 'Having myself married the previous year, this makes me just old enough to be your Mama, and so I shall take you for my son…'

Lady Susanna clasped her hands and, still smiling at the marble putti, she warmed herself on the joy she had given her English visitor. Like the rare pear trees outside in the orchard, she had weathered many storms.

Lady Susanna Kennedy (Montgomerie), Countess of Eglinton (1690-1780) painted by Gavin Hamilton (1723-1798). Reproduced with kind permission of The National Trust for Scotland, Culzean Castle.

BOUT THIS TALE

Lady Susanna Montgomerie née Kennedy, Countess of Eglinton (1689-1780), was born at Culzean Castle near Ayr and became the third wife of the 9th Earl of Eglinton, Alexander Montgomerie, in 1708. Together they had eleven children and Lady Susanna outlived eight of them.

After the death of her husband in 1729, the Countess retired to Auchans Castle, gifted to her by her son Alexander, the 10th Earl of Eglinton. The 10th Earl was indeed murdered by the exciseman Mungo Campbell whom he caught poaching on Eglinton land near Ardrossan in 1769. Campbell later hanged himself before his trial started in Edinburgh.

Lady Susanna was revered as a great beauty and intellect in her day, and several duels were fought in her honour. Able to speak French, German and Italian, she was interested in philosophy and science. She was also a literary patron, an accomplished flute player, and oversaw the family businesses.

This story contains a number of her own words edited from her private correspondence, as well as from James Boswell's and Fanny Burney's diary entries.

On 1st November 1773, James Boswell and Dr Samuel Johnson visited the Countess en route to Boswell's family home in Auchinleck. Lady Susanna then adopted Dr Johnson as her son at the end of the visit. She was also rumoured to have kept and trained a number of rats.

Sadly, the Auchans pear tree was destroyed during a storm in the 1790s.

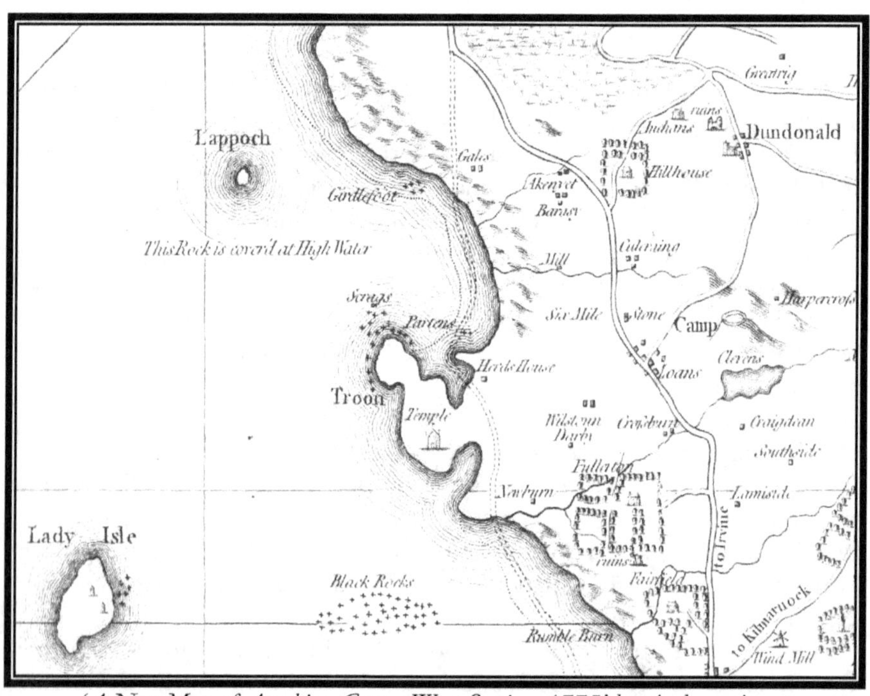

'A New Map of Ayrshire, Centre West Section, 1775' by Andrew Armstrong *(1700-1794). Reproduced with kind permission of the National Library of Scotland.*

ABOUT THE WRITER

Born in 1975, Suzy A. Kelly's work is rooted in the folklore, history, and languages of Scotland. Whilst recovering from ME/CFS, she achieved undergraduate awards in Scottish Cultural Studies and Humanities and is in the final year of her MLitt in Creative Writing at the University of Glasgow.

After decades of living in the Hebrides and Edinburgh, she is now back in Dundonald, where she was born. She lives with her pet Northumbrian, two cats, and a bearded collie called Wooster.

Prose winner of the 2017 Imprint Writing Awards, she is featured in the British Fantasy Society's *Emerging Horizons* anthology and Digital Short Story Project in 2018.

To keep up-to-date with Suzy's forthcoming projects, please join her mailing list at the website below.

www.suzyakelly.com

ABOUT THE ILLUSTRATOR

Michael Kelly was born in Northumberland in 1976. He began working as a mixed media installation artist, exhibiting across the United Kingdom, and is now an illustrator.

Michael's work has been published in online journals and he is a PhD candidate at the Glasgow School of Art. His first graphic novel will be released in June 2018.

https://michaelandrewkelly.weebly.com

BIBLIOGRAPHY

The Baba Witch:
Afanasiev, A. (1985) *The Three Kingdoms: Russian Folktales*. Moscow: Raduga.

Bettelheim, B. (1991) *The Uses of Enchantment: The Meaning and Importance of Fairy Tales*. London: Penguin.

Burke, E. (1823) *A Philosophical Inquiry into the Origin of Our Ideas of the Sublime and Beautiful*. London: Thomas McLean.

Forrester, S. (2013) *Baba Yaga: The Wild Witch of the East in Russian Fairy Tales*. Mississippi: University Press of Mississippi.

Littlewood, N. A. (2017). *A Revision of Invertebrate Features of Designated Sites in Scotland* [Online]. Scottish Natural Heritage Commissioned Report No. 1007. Available from <https://tinyurl.com/y9o5sggy> [Accessed 3rd April 2018].

Ralston, W. R. S. (1873) 'Vasilissa The Fair' in Ralston, W. R. S. (1873) *Russian Folk-tales*. London: Smith, Elder & Co. pp.150-163.

Walker, B. G. (1988) *The Crone: Woman of Age, Wisdom, and Power*. London: HarperCollins.

Warner, M. (2014) *Once Upon a Time: A Short History of Fairy Tale*. Oxford: Oxford University Press.

Zipes, J. (2012) *Fairy Tales and the Art of Subversion*. London: Routledge.

Ae Fond Kiss:
Bennett, M. (1992) *Scottish Customs from the Cradle to the Grave*. Edinburgh: Polygon.

Burns, R. (1791) 'Ae Fond Kiss, And Then We Sever' in *Poems and Songs of Robert Burns* [Online].
Available from <www.gutenberg.org/files/1279/1279-0.txt> [Accessed 23rd March 2018].

Campbell, J. G. (1910) 'The Origin of the Fairy Creed' in *The Scottish Historical Review* [Online]. Vol. 7(28), pp.364-376. Available from <www.jstor.org/stable/25518239> [Accessed 1st April 2018].

Canmore, National Record of the Historic Environment (2018) *Dundonald Castle* [Online].
Available from <https://canmore.org.uk/site/41970/dundonald-castle> [Accessed 1st April 2018].

Christison, D. (1893) 'The prehistoric forts of Ayrshire' in *Proc Soc Antiq Scot*, Vol. 27, pp. 390-1.

Cowan, E. J. & Henderson, L. (eds.) (2001) *A History of Medieval Life in Scotland, 1000 to 1600*. Edinburgh: Edinburgh University Press.

Finlayson, B. (1998) *Wild Harvesters: The First People in Scotland*. Edinburgh: Canongate.

Fyfe, J.G. (ed.) (1928) *Scottish Diaries and Memoirs, 1550 – 1746*. Stirling: Eneas MacKay.

Goodare, J. (2012) 'The Cult of the Seelie Wights in Scotland' in *Folklore* [Online]. Vol. 123(2), pp.198-219. Available from <www.jstor.org/stable/41721541> [Accessed 1st April 2018].

Grinsell, L. V. (1937) 'Some Aspects of the Folklore of Prehistoric Monuments' in *Folklore* [Online]. Vol. 48(3), pp.245-259. Available from <www.jstor.org/stable/1257057> [Accessed 1st April 2018].

Heal, B. and Grell, O.P. (eds.) (2016) *The Impact of the European Reformation: Princes, Clergy and People*. Abingdon: Routledge.

Henderson, L. (ed.) (2009) *Fantastical Imaginations: The Supernatural in Scottish History and Culture*. Edinburgh: Birlinn.

Kirk, R. (2008) *The Secret Commonwealth of Elves, Fauns and Fairies*. New York: Dover Publications.

Love, D. (2009) *Legendary Ayrshire: Custom, Folklore, Tradition*. Auchinleck: Carn Publishing.

Miller, J. (2000) *Myth and Magic: Scotland's Ancient Beliefs & Sacred Places*. Musselburgh: Goblinshead.

Murdoch, G. (2004) *Beyond Calvin: The Intellectual, Political, and Cultural World of Europe's Reformed Churches c. 1540 - 1620*. Hampshire: Palgrave MacMillan.

Paton, H. (ed.) (1936) *Dundonald Parish Records: The Session Book of Dundonald 1602 – 1731.* Edinburgh: Private Publisher.

The Geneva Bible (2007) *A Facsimile of the 1560 Version.* Hendrickson: Massachusetts.

Devil of Loudoun Hill:
Dalyell, J. G. (1834) *The Darker Superstitions of Scotland, Illustrated from History and Practice.* Edinburgh: Waugh and Innes.

Goodare, J. et al (2003) *The Survey of Scottish Witchcraft* [Online]. Available from <www.shca.ed.ac.uk/witches> [Accessed 17th March 2018].

Larner, C., Lee, C. H., McLachland, H. V. (eds.) (2005) *A Source-book of Scottish Witchcraft.* Glasgow: Grimsay Press.

Larner, C. (1983) *Enemies of God.* Oxford: Basil Blackwell.

MacDonald, S. (2002) 'Torture and the Scottish Witch-hunt: A Re-examination' in *International Review of Scottish Studies* [Online]. Vol. 27. Available from
 <www.irss.uoguelph.ca/index.php/irss/article/view/199/234> [Accessed 8th April 2018].

Melville, R. D. (1905) 'The Use and Forms of Judicial Torture in England and Scotland' in *The Scottish Historical Review* [Online]. Vol. 2(7). pp.225-248. Available from <www.jstor.org/stable/25517609> [Accessed 8th April 2018].

Miller, J. (2005) *Magic and Witchcraft in Scotland.* Musselburgh: Goblinshead.

Neil, W. N. (1922) 'The Professional Pricker and His Test for Witchcraft' in *The Scottish Historical Review* [Online]. Vol. 19(75), pp.205-213. Available from <ww.jstor.org/stable/25519442> [Accessed 8th April 2018].

Paton, H. (ed.) (1936) *Dundonald Parish Records: The Session Book of Dundonald 1602 – 1731.* Edinburgh: Private Publisher.

Pitcairn, R. (1833) *Ancient Criminal Trials in Scotland: Vol. 2.* Edinburgh: William Tait.

Row, J. (1841) *The History of the Kirk of Scotland: From the Year 1558 to 1637*. Edinburgh: Wodrow Society.

Smout, T.C. (1985) *A History of the Scottish People 1560-1830*. London: Fontana Press.

Ait the Smuggler's Grave:
Cullen, L. M. (1989) *Smuggling and the Ayrshire Economic Boom of the 1760s and 1770s*. Darvel: Walker & Connell Ltd.

Galt, J. (1821) *Annals of the Parish*. Edinburgh: William Blackwood & Sons.

Kay, B. (2006) *Scots: The Mither Tongue*. Edinburgh: Mainstream Publishing.

MacLeod, I. (ed.) (1990) *The Scots Thesaurus*. Aberdeen: Aberdeen University Press.

Mayes, B. (2018) *Dundonald Graveyard* [Online]. Available from <www.dundonald-parish-church.com> [Accessed 20th February 2018].

McClure, J. D. (1988) *Why Scots Matters*. Edinburgh: The Saltire Society.

Robinson, M. (ed.) (1996) *The Concise Scots Dictionary*. Edinburgh: Chambers.

Scotland [504] in *The Scots Magazine* 1739-1803. Vol. 42, pp. 553-556.

Steele, W. (1833) *A Summary of the Powers and Duties of Juries in Criminal Trials in Scotland*. Edinburgh: Thomas Clark.

South Ayrshire Libraries (2012) *The Gibbet Stones from Ayr's Sandgate Tolbooth* [Online]. Available from <https://southayrshirehistory.wordpress.com/2012/09/04/the-gibbet-stones-from-ayrs-sandgate-tolbooth/> [26th February 2018].

Troon and District Family History Society (1994) *Dundonald: Monumental Inscriptions*. Troon: Troon and District Family History Society

Wilkins, F. (2007) *The Smugglers of Kyle*. Kidderminster: Wyre Forest Press.

Wilkins, F. (2008) *The Loans Smugglers*. Ayr: Ayrshire Archaeological and Natural History Society.

Wilkins, F. (2008) *Matthew Hay: Smuggler, Farmer, and Poisoner?* Kidderminster: Wyre Forest Press.

The Auchans Pear:
Bingham, K. (2017) *Lady Susanna, Countess of Eglinton (1689-1780)* [Online]. Available from <https://culzeancastleandcountrypark.wordpress.com> [Accessed 20th February 2018].

Boswell, J. (2014) *Boswell's Life of Johnson. Vol. 5: The Tour to the Hebrides and the Journey into North Wales* [Online]. Available from <www.oxfordscholarlyeditions.com> [Accessed 20th February 2018].

Fraser, W. (1859) *Memorials of the Montgomeries, Earls of Eglinton.* Edinburgh: publisher unknown.

Gillespie, J. (1939) *Dundonald: A Contribution to Parochial History.* Glasgow: John Wylie & Co.

Graham, H. (1884) *The Fruit Manual: A Guide to the Fruits and Fruit Trees of Great Britain.* London: Journal of Horticulture.

Graham, H. (1908) A *Group of Scottish Women.* Duffield & Company: New York.

Marshall, R. K. (2004) *Lady Susanna Montgomerie* [Online]. Available from <www.oxforddnb.com> [Accessed 20th February 2018].

Woolsey, S. C. (ed.) (1910) *The Diary and Letters of Frances Burney (Madame d'Arblay).* Boston: Little, Brown, and Company.